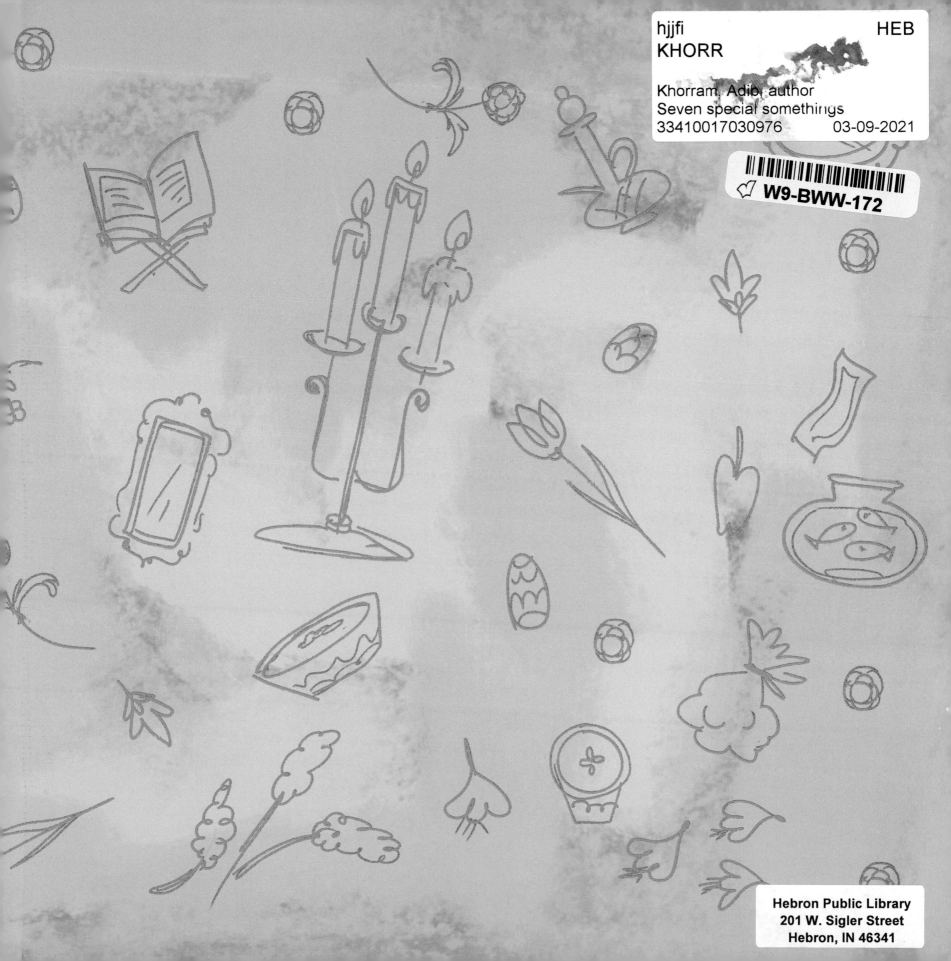

Seven Special Somethings

A NOWRUZ STORY

by
ADIB KHORRAM

illustrated by
ZAINAB FAIDHI

🏛 DIAL BOOKS FOR YOUNG READERS

For my family.
—A.K.

**To my Kurdish and Persian friends
who love celebrating Nowruz,
and to my family.**
—Z.F.

DIAL BOOKS FOR YOUNG READERS

An imprint of Penguin Random House LLC, New York

First published in the United States of America by Dial Books for Young Readers,
an imprint of Penguin Random House LLC, 2021

Text copyright © 2021 by Adib Khorram
Illustrations copyright © 2021 by Zainab Faidhi

Visit us online at penguinrandomhouse.com.

Library of Congress Cataloging-in-Publication Data is available.

Manufactured in China • ISBN 9780593108260

1 3 5 7 9 10 8 6 4 2

Design by Jason Henry • Text set in Quire Sans Pro

Kian ran down the stairs laughing.
It was the first day of spring, and Nowruz was here at last!

While Maman and Baba cooked and cleaned all day, Kian was allowed to help.

It was Kian's job to match the socks.
And beat the rugs. And even vacuum.

The sofreh haft-seen was set in the living room.

"Maman," Kian said. "Why are there only seven things on the haft-seen?"

"It's tradition, Kian."

Sabzeh (sprouts)
FOR REBIRTH

Serkeh (vinegar)
FOR PATIENCE

Seer (garlic)
FOR HEALTH

"Nowruz is the start of spring," Maman said, "when everything is new again. The Seven S's on the table are symbols. We hope they will make us happy in the new year."

Sekkeh (coins)
FOR WEALTH

Sib (apple)
FOR BEAUTY

Samanoo (pudding)
FOR BRAVERY

Sumaq (spice)
FOR SUNSHINE

Maman went back to cooking, and Baba left for the airport to pick up Khanumjan and Aghajan.

Kian studied the table.

"Why only seven symbols? If I found more S's, could I make our new year even happier?"

"Sonny starts with S. What will Sonny bring us in the new year?"

Kian tried to put the table back together, but the vinegar had spilled, and the coins had rolled under the couch.

"I have to find new *S*'s for the table. *Sonny*'s not the only thing that begins with *S*!"

Kian searched and searched. In his room, under his bed, he finally found something.

"Sugar for sweetness! I wonder what Maman is making for dessert."

Kian snuck into his parents' room.
Surely they had some things that began with S.

"Maman's soap! It smells so good. Like one of Maman's hugs."

"Baba's sneakers! These don't smell so good.
But Baba needs them to run and play with me!"

In the guest room, he found a bowl of Aghajan's favorite snack.

"Aghajan's watermelon seeds! These will keep our bellies full in the new year. I wonder if we roasted enough?"

One of Khanumjan's scarves was hanging over the rocking chair where she liked to sit and read to Kian.

"Khanumjan's scarf! That starts with S! This will keep us warm in the new year!"

Kian put everything on the new haft-seen, but he only counted six *S*'s. He was still arranging things when Baba came home with his grandparents.

Khanumjan said, "Look how much you've grown!"
And Aghajan asked, "What are you making?"
"A new haft-seen. Sonny and I broke the old one."

Baba laughed. "It's a different kind of haft-seen, Kian.
But look! It shows our whole family."

"It's not done yet. I still have to find a seventh S."
But then Maman called them all to eat.
"Noosh-e jan!"

The table was full of Kian's favorites: fish, and rice, and Persian pickles, and hot tea. Kian's fingers got sticky from all the baklava he ate.

But he couldn't stop thinking about the seventh S.

After dinner, Baba gathered them
all together to take a picture with
Kian's new haft-seen.

"I wish I had found a seventh S."

"Don't worry, Kian," Aghajan said.

"You did a good job," Khanumjan said.

Maman hugged Kian. "It's a beautiful haft-seen."

"Everybody smile!"

"Smile?"

Kian looked up at his happy family.

"*Smile* starts with S! This will make us happiest of all in the new year!"

AUTHOR'S NOTE

Every year, around March 21, Persian people—people from the area where Iran is now—celebrate the start of a new year. In Farsi, the Persian language, *Nowruz* (or *Nawruz* or *Norouz*) means "new day." It's the celebration of the start of spring, a time for growth and rebirth.

One of the best parts of Nowruz is the sofreh haft-seen each family sets. *Haft* is the Farsi word for the number 7, and *sin* is the Farsi letter for S. The seven S's on the table can change from family to family, and many add extra items to the table, symbols of renewal like eggs, goldfish, or sacred texts.

But at its heart, Nowruz isn't about tables, or S's, or food. It's about gathering together with the people you love to wish for happiness in the coming year.

Eid-e shomaa mobarak!